Judy Moody & Stink

THE MAD, MAD, MAD, MAD TREASURE HUNT

Books by Megan McDonald and Peter H. Reynolds

Judy Moody
Judy Moody Gets Famous!
Judy Moody Saves the World!
Judy Moody Predicts the Future
Judy Moody: The Doctor Is In!
Judy Moody Declares Independence!
Judy Moody: Around the World in 8 1/2 Days
Judy Moody Goes to College
Judy Moody, Girl Detective
Judy Moody and the NOT Bummer Summer
Judy Moody and the Bad Luck Charm

Stink: The Incredible Shrinking Kid
Stink and the Incredible Super-Galactic Jawbreaker
Stink and the World's Worst Super-Stinky Sneakers
Stink and the Great Guinea Pig Express
Stink: Solar System Superhero
Stink and the Ultimate Thumb-Wrestling Smackdown
Stink and the Midnight Zombie Walk
Stink and the Freaky Frog Freakout
Stink and the Shark Sleepover

Stink-O-Pedia: Super Stinky-y Stuff From A to Zzzzz
Stink-O-Pedia 2: Super Stinky-y Stuff From A to Z

Judy Moody & Stink: The Holly Joliday
Judy Moody & Stink: The Mad, Mad, Mad, Mad Treasure Hunt

Books by Megan McDonald

The Sisters Club
The Sisters Club: Rule of Three
The Sisters Club: Cloudy with a Chance of Boys

Books by Peter H. Reynolds

The Dot • Ish • So Few of Me • Rose's Garden
Sky Colour • The Smallest Gift of Christmas

www.judymoody.com   www.stinkmoody.com

Judy Moody & Stink

THE MAD, MAD, MAD, MAD TREASURE HUNT

Here lies
the treasure

X

Megan McDonald

illustrated by Peter H. Reynolds

WALKER
BOOKS

4 6 8 10 9 7 5 3

Text © 2009 Megan McDonald
Illustrations © 2009 Peter H. Reynolds
Judy Moody font © 2004 Peter H. Reynolds

Judy Moody ™. Judy Moody is a registered trademark of Candlewick Press, Inc.

The right of Megan McDonald and Peter H. Reynolds to be identified as
author and illustrator respectively of this work has been asserted by them
in accordance with the Copyright, Designs and Patents Act 1988

This book has been typeset in Stone Informal

Printed in Malaysia

British Library Cataloguing in Publication Data:
a catalogue record for this book is available from the British Library

ISBN 978-1-4063-1980-4

www.walker.co.uk

For Eliza
M. M.

For Holly McGhee
P. H. R.

CONTENTS

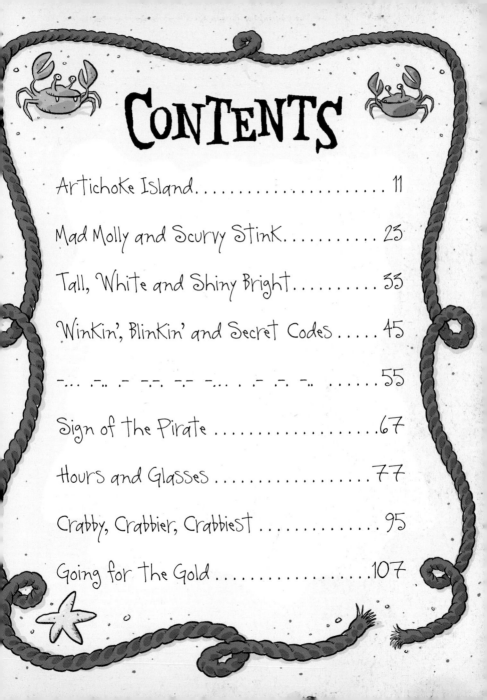

WHO'S WHO

MAD MOLLY O'MAGGOT
AKA JUDY MOODY

SCURVY STINK
AKA STINK MOODY

SCURVY SAM
AKA CAP'N WEEVIL

CAP'N FLAPJACK SCUPPERDECK
AKA DAD

CRIMSON KATE MOPBUCKET
AKA MUM

SHOUTIN' HAYLEY DAGGER
AKA SMART GIRL

JELLYBONES KNEEKNOCKER
AKA TALL BOY

As long as ships have sailed the seas, there have been pirates. And as long as there have been pirates, Stink Moody has wanted to sail on a ship to an island. A *treasure* island.

A ferry boat wasn't exactly a pirate ship – but still! Stink reached into his survival kit (aka his backpack). Compass, torch, small notebook, *Treasure Island*, pirate flag, pirate rule book … spyglass!

From the upper deck of the ferry, Stink peered through his spyglass with one eye.

The eye not covered with a pirate patch, that is.

All he could see was blue, blue, blue. Blue sky. Blue water. Blue ... T-shirt? His sister, Judy Moody, was blocking his view.

"Hey, Judy. You make a better door than a window."

When Judy moved, Stink focused his spyglass on the horizon. "I think I can see it," he said. "Vegetable Island! I mean, Artichoke Island."

"You mean Ocracoke Island," Judy corrected him.

"Whatever," said Stink. "I just want to meet pirates and look at shipwrecks and see real gold and find treasure."

"Yeah, right. We're only in North Carolina for a few days."

Through his spyglass Stink spotted Mum and Dad down on the lower deck. "Ahoy! You there, on the poop deck," he called.

"What's the poop deck? Wait, that's where all the seagulls poop, right? Let me look." Judy grabbed the spyglass from Stink.

Stink swung his arms in the air and sang like a pirate:

"Fifteen men on the dead man's chest –
Yo-ho-ho, and a bucket of fun!"

"Hey, Stink, there's a boy on the poop deck staring up at you. That tall one wearing the turtle T-shirt. Next to that girl with the glasses. She looks smart. And she's staring at you too."

Stink sliced the air with his invisible sword.

"Fifteen chests on the dead man's bum –
Yo-ho-ho, and a packet of gum!"

He pretended to walk the plank on the upper deck. The boat hit a bunch of waves. Judy hung on tight to the rail. Stink slumped to the deck, making pukey stomach-ache faces.

"What's wrong?" Judy asked. "Are you going to puke?"

"*Arrr!* Never say 'puke' when a pirate's about to puke."

Judy tried to think of something –
anything – to take Stink's mind off the
pukes. A joke! "Stink. What do you call
pirate throw-up?"

"I said please DON'T say 'puke'."

"I didn't say 'puke'. I said 'throw-up'."

"You're like the Girl Who Cried
Throw-Up or something."

"OK, then what do you call pirate
heave-ho?" said Judy.

"I call it *gross*," said Stink.

"No, you call it pieces o'ate!" Judy
laughed herself silly.

"My feet itch." Stink scratched his feet
like mad. "And my teeth hurt. Do I have
red blotches on me? Are my teeth falling
out?"

"Stick out your tongue and say *ARRR*," said Doctor Judy. "Stink, you're already missing two teeth, and your face is sunburned."

"Tummy-ache. Feet itch. Teeth falling out. Red face. *And* I'm grumpy."

"I'll say."

"That's it. I have it."

"Have what?"

"Scurvy!" said Stink. "I'm dead."

"Scurvy!" said Judy. "You're just a little seasick. Close your eyes for a minute and put your head between your knees. Here, Mum gave me crackers in case we felt like we might hurl."

Stink was quiet for a while, munching on crackers. Finally, when the boat

wasn't rocking any more, he stood up.
"I'm OK now. I feel much better." He even
waved his red Jolly Roger at his parents.

"What's with the red pirate flag,
Stink?" Judy asked.

"For your information, this was the
flag of a real Moody pirate."

"A moody pirate? Rare! But weren't
all pirates pretty grumpy?"

"His name was Christopher Moody.
He sailed around the Carolinas with
Black Bart. He was one of the only
pirates with a red flag. It had a skull and
crossbones, an arm
with a dagger, and
an hourglass with
wings. That means,

'Your time is running out.' Get it?"

"Whoa," said Judy. "A real pirate named Moody? Just think, Stink, Christopher Moody could be like our great-great-great-great-great-grandpa."

"Shiver me timbers!" yelled Stink.

"Rare!" said Judy. "I have pirate blood in me."

"Girls can't be pirates."

"Says who?"

"Says Pirate Rule Number Six: no girls allowed on ships. It's the Pirate Code." Stink pulled out the *Book of Pirate Rules*.

"See? There are ten pirate rules. Break one, and they feed you to the shark*ssss*."

"What about girl pirates like Anne Bonny and Mary Read, who dressed up like boys? Take that, Pirate Rule Number Six."

"Hey, don't be knocking the pirate rules."

"I read about a girl pirate who had her ear bitten off in a fight. She picked up her chewed-off ear and wore it on a chain round her neck. No lie."

Stink lifted up Judy's hair. "Looks to me like you still have both your ears," he said. "And the only thing round your neck is the shark-tooth necklace that I gave you."

"Avast, ye hairy carbuncle. Ye be spit on the scab of life, ye scurvy nuncle!"

"Land, ho!" called Stink as the ferry pulled up to the dock. He ran down the gangplank, singing like Captain Hook:

"Yo ho, yo ho, the frisky plank,
You walks along it so."

His legs felt all wibbly-wobbly.

"Still got yer sea legs on, I see," said a voice from the dock. A *scurvy* voice.

"Huh?" Stink looked up, squinting.

A large shadow blotted out the sun. The shadow had a dirty kerchief and a scraggly beard. The shadow had an eyepatch and a gold hoop earring.

The shadow was a pirate!

"Name's Cap'n Weevil," said the pirate. "But me friends call me Scurvy Sam."

"I think I had scurvy on the ferry!" said Stink.

"And who might ye be?"

"Um, Cap'n Moody, here," said Stink, pointing to himself.

"But his friends call him Scurvy Stink," Judy teased, coming up behind him.

"And this be Mad Molly O'Maggot." Stink pointed to Judy.

"Thanks a lot," she murmured.

"Welcome to Pirate Island," said Scurvy Sam, winking his one eye.

"Pirate Island? I thought this was Okey-Dokey Island," said Stink.

The pirate laughed. "Folks 'round here call it Pirate Island, on account o' Blackbeard himself haunting these parts back in the day."

"Whoa," said Stink. "Are you a for-real pirate? I mean, are ye?"

"O' course I'm real. Yank me beard if ye like, mate."

"Um, no thanks." Pirate Rule Number Eleven: do NOT get on the wrong side of a pirate, or he might just take your head off.

"Get yer maps here," Scurvy Sam called to people getting off the ferry. He handed one to Judy.

"Listen up, all ye scum buckets and scallywags," Scurvy Sam announced.

"This be the weekend of the Third Annual Pirate Island Treasure Hunt. Fun and mayhem start first thing in the morn."

"Really?" asked Stink.

"Really?" asked Judy.

"Would I lie t' ye?" asked the pirate.

"O' course," said Judy. "Yer a pirate."

"Ye got me there, lassie, but I'm not pulling yer leg this time. C'mon down to me pirate ship at Silver Lake Harbor. X marks the spot." He pointed to a big red X on the map. "I be givin' out the first clue to the treasure at  ten hundred hours sharp. That'll give ye time to grub up and to catch forty winks before morn."

"What do we have to do?" Stink asked.

"Follow the trail of clues, laddie. First to collect sixteen pieces o' eight wins the gold doubloon."

"A doubloon is a gold coin," Stink told Judy. "It takes sixteen pieces of eight – silver dollars – to make one doubloon."

"I knew that," said Judy, even though she didn't.

"A pirate doubloon!" said Stink. "Is it real gold?"

"As gold as a pirate's tooth," Scurvy Sam joked. "If ye win, ye get a ride with me aboard Blackbeard's own pirate ship, the *Queen Anne's Revenge II*. If ye dare."

"Sounds like a barrel o' fun," said Stink.

"'Tain't easy," said Scurvy Sam. "Where there's pirates, there be tricks and tons of monkey business. *Yarr.*"

Dad walked up with their luggage. "C'mon. Time to get to the inn."

"And wash up before we grub up," said Mum, wheeling a suitcase.

"Did you hear?" said Stink. "A real treasure hunt. Right here on Pirate Island. Can we do it?"

"Can we, can we, can we?" asked Mad Molly and Scurvy Stink.

⚓ ⚓ ⚓

"Lights out at eight o'clock," Mum said when they got back to the Clam On Inn after supper. "That goes for torches too. Pirate Rule Number Four."

"Not you too!" Judy groaned. "We're on holiday. Can't we stay up late? Bedtime isn't a pirate rule."

"No mutiny on the SS *Moody*," Mum said, shaking her head.

Stink checked the pirate rule book. "She's right."

"C'mon, kids. We've had a long trip today," said Dad. "You'll want to have lots of energy for tomorrow's—"

"Treasure hunt!" screamed Judy and Stink at the same time.

Before they knew it, the two of them were catching forty winks.

Stink was the first one out of bed the next morning.

"Stink, you're wearing that striped pirate T-shirt *again*? Didn't you even have a bath?"

"Pirates don't have baths," said Stink. "Here, smell my armpit."

"Gross! You smell worse than a pirate's monkey on a poop deck!"

"*Yarr,*" said Stink.

After Mum and Dad had woken up, drunk buckets of coffee and read the paper for a year, they took Judy and

Stink to Silver Lake Harbor, where the treasure hunt was about to begin.

"I see it!" said Stink. "I see the pirate ship!"

Before them loomed the tall poles of the three-masted square-rigger, the *Queen Anne's Revenge II*. Sails flapped like kites in the wind. Kids and families gazed up at the ship in awe.

A ship's bell clanged several times in a row. Just then, a pirate swung down on a long rope from the yardarm (like Tarzan) and landed on deck with a loud *ker-PLUNK* (not like Tarzan). It was Scurvy Sam!

"Ahoy, ahoy, all ye treasure seekers," he called. "Welcome to the Third Annual

Pirate Island Treasure Hunt. Listen up, scallywags. There be five clues in all. Each clue'll lead ye to the next. When ye think ye figgered out a clue, turn it in to the nearest Assistant Pirate. They be wearin' a red sash and givin' out pieces o' eight. First one to figger out all five clues and turn in sixteen pieces o' eight wins the gold doubloon and a ride with me on the *QAR II*."

Scurvy Sam held up a silver piece of eight. "I'll be givin' ye yer first piece o' eight. The last one is hidden, and it be harder to find than a bow tie on a pirate."

Everybody laughed.

"If ye be the one to find it, make haste back to me at Pirate Headquarters. No wooden nickels allowed!" Scurvy Sam cackled. "One last thing – ye have until noon tomorrow. When ye hear the ship's bell, c'mon back to see if anybody won the gold. Everybody who joins in goes home with loot – a big bag o' pirate booty."

After a lot more *ahoys*, *avasts* and *aye ayes*, Scurvy Sam unrolled a parchment and read aloud the first clue for all to hear.

Clue 1

Tall as a tree,
dressed in white,
my bridal veil
is shiny bright.
Up all night,
never sleeping;
if I rest,
many are weeping.
Upon these shores
since days of old,
my silent message
points to gold.

"Good luck t' ye. May ye have strong winds at yer back, only bilge rats for enemies and a barrel o' fun. Let the plunderin' begin!"

Judy and Stink said goodbye to Mum and Dad.

"Dad and I are going to the beach.

If we don't see you before noon, we'll meet you in front of Barnacle Bob's hot-dog stand at twelve thirty," Mum said.

"Have fun!" said Dad.

Stink and Judy pushed their way through the crowd, past the big bald man with a small boy on his shoulders, past the lady with three dogs, past the twin kids with ice lollies. When they got to the front, Scurvy Sam was handing out the first piece of eight and the first clue. A girl with braces stepped on Stink's foot while reaching for her coin.

"Stink, don't look now. It's Tall Boy and Smart Girl. The ones from the ferry yesterday." Judy cast a squinty-eyed look their way.

"Hurry up. Read the clue again," said Stink. "We have to beat them."

They read the clue three times.

"'Tall as a tree,'" said Stink. "It's got to be the pirate ship. The masts are as tall as a tree, and the sails could be the bride's thingy."

"It can't be the ship. Nobody's even allowed on the ship unless you win the gold."

"Then I think it's a flagpole. A flagpole is as tall as a tree."

"Well, I saw a church in town, and it has a tall steeple. And it's white. A flagpole isn't dressed in white."

"It is if it's been painted white," said Stink. "Like the one I saw in front of the post office."

"But it doesn't have a bridal veil," said Judy.

"It does if it's flying a *white* flag," Stink said.

"All I know is that churches have brides."

Judy was right. Churches did have brides. What a bilge rat!

"And you could say churches are up all night," said Judy. "You know, they're always open in case people need them."

"Flagpoles are up all night too," said Stink.

"But they take the flag down at the end of the day."

"Scum buckets!" Stink said. Judy was right again. "But what about the weeping? People cry when somebody dies, and the flag is put at half mast."

Stink had a point.

"But people cry in churches too," Judy said. "Like at a wedding. I say *church*."

"Flagpole," said Stink.

"*Church.*"

"FLAGPOLE!"

"Hey! I call Pirate Rule Number Eight. No fighting," said Judy.

"That's only aboard ship," said Stink.

"I give in," said Judy. "Let's go to *both* places."

Judy craned her neck and squinted up at the flagpole outside the post office. "Stink, this flag isn't white."

"It's white *between* the red stripes," said Stink.

"Oh, brother. C'mon, let's go to the church," said Judy. But when they got to the church, it was locked.

"Aha! So it's *not* up all night," said Stink.

"At least it's tall and white and has brides," said Judy. But no Assistant Pirate with a sash was anywhere in sight.

"Think. What else is tall?" Stink looked up, down and all around. He saw the lighthouse sticking out of the trees. "A lighthouse is tall!"

"And painted white!" said Judy.

"And it has a light that is shiny bright!" said Stink.

"And it's up all night!" said Judy. "And if it stops, ships will crash onto the rocks."

"To the lighthouse!" said Stink, pointing the way.

⚓ ⚓ ⚓

The lighthouse stood tall, blinking in the sun. Stink squinted to read the plaque. "This lighthouse is so old."

"I know," said Judy.

"It's almost two hundred years old,"
said Stink.

"I know."

"This lighthouse is so tall," said Stink.

"I know."

"It's like twenty-three metres tall."

"I know."

"King Kong was only eight metres tall."

"I know."

"You can see the light if you're twenty-three kilometres away at sea."

"I know."

"They used to have to light it like a candle wick, in whale oil."

"I know."

"Every lighthouse has its own pattern of blinks, so ships will know where they are," said Stink.

"I— What?"

"Some even use Morse code. Didn't you know?" asked Stink.

"No, I didn't know lighthouses blinked

out a secret message in *Morse code*. Rare!"
said Judy. "Stink, you're a genius."

"So how do we find the next clue?"
he asked.

Judy wasn't listening. She was
watching Tall Boy and Smart Girl
talking to a park keeper. A park keeper
wearing a pirate sash! "Let's go and talk
to that lady Assistant Pirate."

The park keeper had short curly
hair and a Smokey the Bear hat. She
smiled at Judy and Stink. "What's the
password?" she whispered.

"Um … lighthouse?" they whispered
at the same time.

"You just earned five pieces o' eight!"

Five! The keeper reached into a bucket and poured coins into Stink's hands. They jingled all the way.

Stink dug into his backpack, pulled out a shiny red pouch and tied it to his belt. "This'll be for all our pirate booty. We have six already!"

"Ye better guard that booty with your life," said the keeper. "There be pirates all over these parts!" Then she handed them the next clue.

Judy and Stink sat on a driftwood log and opened the clue.

-... .-.. .- -.-. -.- -... . .- .-. -..

"It's in Morse code!" said Stink.

"Morse code? Oh no! We won't have a clue what this means."

"Who says?" Stink reached into his survival backpack again.

"*Shh!*" said Judy. "Spies on deck. Spies on deck."

"You have the map," they heard Tall Boy tell Smart Girl. "Where's the library?"

"The library!" Judy whispered. "Good idea. Let's go—"

Stink held up a spiral notebook with MORSE CODE on the cover.

"You have Morse code in your survival kit?" Judy asked.

"You never know when you might get marooned on a desert island, like Gilligan's Island, and have to send out a rescue signal."

"Stink, have I told you lately you're a genius?"

Stink grinned. "You just did. But tell me again."

Judy looked up each letter of the coded message, writing them down in Stink's notebook as she found them.

"What is it? What does it say?" Stink pestered.

"Let me finish," said Judy.

"It's *Badbear*," said Stink. *"Blabear? Blackbird? Blackbear?"*

"BLACKBEARD!" screamed Judy and Stink at the same time, forgetting all about spies.

Judy and Stink met Mum and Dad in front of Barnacle Bob's. "Those two girls with painted faces have maps too," said Judy, pointing.

"So does that surfer-dude kid," said Stink. "And *he's* not stopping to eat hot dogs."

Judy and Stink wolfed down hot dogs, then their parents drove them all over town while they tried to solve the next clue. Something about Blackbeard.

They went to Blackbeard's Castle.

They peeked inside a gift shop called Blackbeard's Folly. They checked out Barefoot Blackbeard, a surf shop. But all they found were a lot of flip-flops.

"Let's park and walk into the centre of town," said Mum. "I need to get some suntan lotion. And I'm hoping to find some art supplies so we—"

"Do we have to?" asked Stink. He could already feel his feet falling off from all the boring old shopping.

"C'mon – it'll be fun," said Mum.

"There's a toy store, and a pet shop like Fur & Fangs, and an ice-cream place."

"Pirates don't play with toys," said Stink. "Or go to pet shops."

"Not even Toys *Arrr* Us?" Mum joked.

"And they definitely don't eat ice cream," said Judy.

"Not even *Marrrs Barrr* Crunch?" Dad teased.

"Sometimes parents are clueless," Judy whispered to Stink.

"We're clue-less too," said Stink.

Judy and Stink laughed till their stomachs hurt.

"Stop!" said Stink. "You're making me get scurvy again."

⚓ ⚓ ⚓

In town, Judy and Stink saw kids with maps everywhere.

"Stink. Across the street. Tall Boy and Smart Girl."

"Are you doing the Girl-Who-Cried-Pelican thing again, where you get me to look?" He looked anyway. "Let's follow them. As in *spy*."

"That's called cheating, Stink."

"Pirate Rule Number Something or Other: cheat every chance you get."

"Car*bunk*le," said Judy.

Judy and Stink trudged up and down Back Road and School Road behind Mum and Dad, in one shop and out another. Stink made bored sounds. Judy made bored faces.

Until … they heard a voice.

"Walk the plank! Walk the plank!" said the voice. It was not a Scurvy Sam pirate voice. It was a high, squeaky voice. "Shiver me timbers! Shiver me timbers!" the voice screeched.

"I think it's coming from the pet shop," said Judy, rushing inside.

"Pet shop!" Stink called to his parents, rushing after Judy.

"Jolly Roger! Pieces of eight! Jolly Roger!"

"It's that parrot!" said Stink, pointing to a large red, yellow and blue bird with long tail feathers. They hurried over to his cage.

"RARE!" said Judy.

"What's your name?" Stink asked in a parrot voice.

"Stink, it says right here that his name is—"

"BLACKBEARD!" Judy and Stink both screamed at the same time.

They rushed over to the teenage boy behind the counter. He had coal-black hair that fell in his eyes, a green army jacket with the sleeves ripped off and a silver hoop earring.

"Maybe *that* guy's Blackbeard," Stink whispered.

"Do you know about the treasure hunt?" Judy asked the boy. "Because we think your parrot is Blackbeard, and that's our next clue."

"You got it," said the kid, putting on his red sash. He pressed a button on the till and handed them four pieces of eight.

"That's ten!" said Stink. "We have ten! We're gonna win! We only need to solve three more clues and get six more pieces of eight."

Stink and Judy went over to the cage again. They looked around for a piece of paper inside the cage, outside the cage, under the cage.

"Hey, there's nothing here," Judy said.

"He has it," the guy said, smiling. "Just ask him."

"*Bwaack!* Blackbeard singing in the dead of night!"

"Hey! He's singing that old Beatles song Dad sings about the blackbird," said Judy. "Maybe the clue's a blackbird."

"Is it a blackbird?" Stink asked the parrot. "Is that the clue?"

"Sign of the pirate. Sign of the pirate," said Blackbeard, ruffling his feathers and bobbing his head up and down.

"He's getting all excited. Maybe 'sign of the pirate' is the clue."

"*Bwaack!* Sign of the pirate."

"That has just got to be it," said Judy. "Every time we say the word *clue*—"

"*Bwaack!* Sign of the pirate."

"There – see what I mean?"

"Yeah, he sounds just like a broken record," said Stink.

"Is it 'sign of the pirate'? Is that the clue?" Judy asked the guy behind the counter.

The guy nodded.

"Sign of the pirate," Blackbeard the parrot squawked again.

"We know! We know!" said Stink, covering his ears. "Let's get out of here. I can't think."

Judy and Stink waited outside while Mum and Dad were in the art shop. A family with two little kids walked past, clutching the first clue.

"They haven't even found the you-know-what yet," Stink whispered.

"But what about *him*?" said Judy. She pointed to a red-haired, freckle-faced boy with white gunk smeared on his nose. "I think I heard his pockets jingling when he walked past. As in *pirate booty*."

Stink wasn't looking. He was busy counting silver coins again.

"Hey, Tall Boy and Smart Girl are going into the smoothie shop," said Judy.

"Do you think they know something we don't know?" Stink asked.

"Not unless the shop has a pirate sign on it somewhere. C'mon, Stink. Think. Get that genius brain humming."

"Maybe they have a special flavour like Shiver Me Timbers ice cream, and that's the sign of a pirate."

"Oh, brother."

"Or else, I think it's got to be a flag," said Stink.

"I think you have flags on the brain," said Judy.

"Yeah, on the *genius* brain," said Stink, cracking up. "I mean a *pirate* flag.

Every pirate has his own sign on his Jolly Roger or Bloody Red."

"Don't look now, but I think *somebody's* spying on us," said Judy.

Across the road, while Smart Girl slurped a smoothie, Tall Boy was looking through binoculars – aimed right at Judy and Stink.

"Those Sneaky Petes," said Stink.

"Let 'em spy," said Judy. "We're not even doing anything."

"Yeah, they're not the only spies on this island," said Stink, taking out his spyglass and pointing it at Tall Boy. "Never mind. They're not even looking at us. Looks like they're spying on the art shop."

"What's the big-whoop deal about the art shop?" asked Judy. "It's just paintbrushes and stuff."

"I think they're checking out every shop on this side of the street. Probably looking for any signs that have pirates on them."

Judy looked up to read the old-timey wooden sign.

"Way rare," she said, pointing at the sign. "Check that out. The sign is in the form of an acrostic – get it? The first letter of each word spells out *PIRATE*. That's got to be it! I just know it! C'mon, Scurvy Stink." Judy yanked her brother by the arm. "Let's hurry and get our next clue before those Nancy Drews beat us."

Ye
Artful
Eye

Paintbrushes
Inks
Rubber Stamps
Art Supplies
Teacher Supplies
Easels

OPEN

The Assistant Pirate at the art shop handed over three more coins – and the next clue.

As they were leaving, Tall Boy and Smart Girl crossed the road, heading for the art shop. Judy and Stink ducked in a doorway and bent their heads over the next clue.

Clue 4

Nary a tick,
nary a tock –
silent, silent,
the handless clock.

Tarry no longer;
cast off all doubt.
The sands of time
are running out.

"Clock!" Stink said in a loud whisper. "It's a clock!"

"But the clue says it doesn't tick or tock," said Judy. "Or have hands. Hey, maybe it's a digital clock – like a watch."

"Let's ask Mum and Dad if there's a place to buy watches around here."

Judy read the clue again. She looked at Stink, who was walking the plank (aka a wooden bench) and waving his pirate flag in the air while they waited for Mum and Dad to catch up.

"Hey, you know that Christopher Moody pirate guy? Didn't he have a saying about time running out?"

"That's what the hourglass stands for on his flag," said Stink. "It means

don't mess with a pirate, or you'll be dead. Wait! An *hourglass* is a clock with no hands! It doesn't tick, and it doesn't tock, and it *doesn't* have hands, and it *does* have sand! The *sands* of time."

"Right you are, matey!" said Judy.

"But where are we going to find an hourglass?" Stink asked.

"Wherever there be dead pirates."

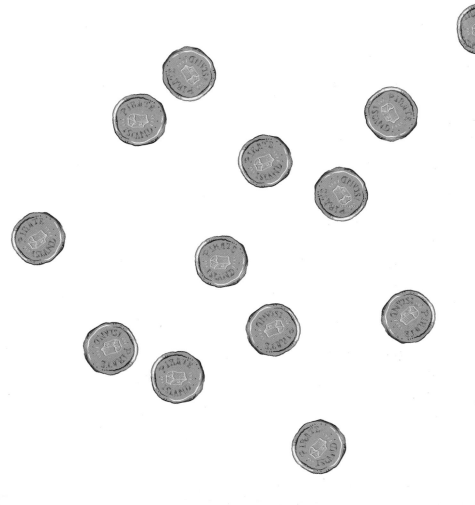

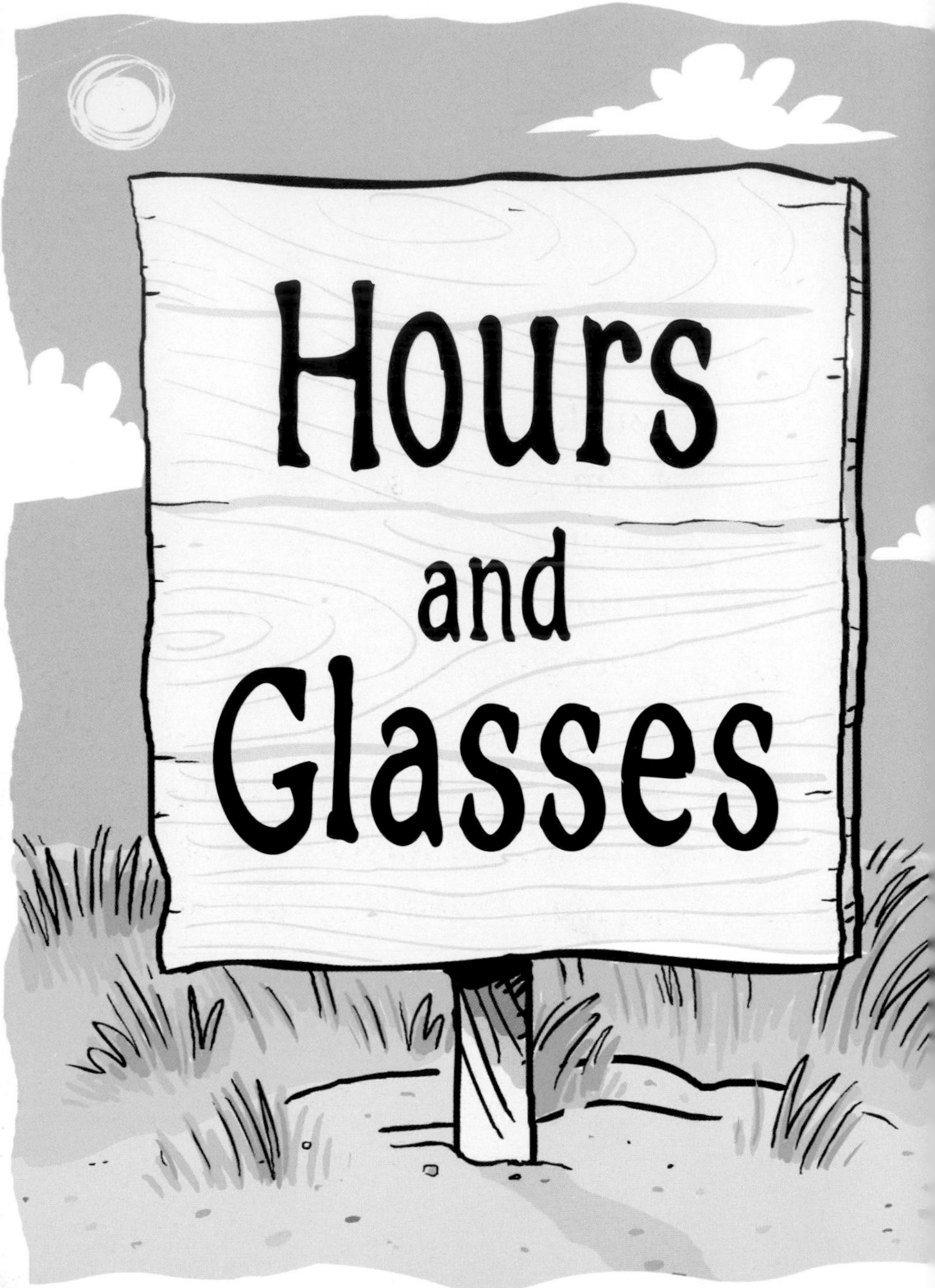
Hours
and
Glasses

"I'm hot," Stink whined.

"Hi, Hot. I'm Thirsty," said Judy, cracking herself up.

"You kids have been at it all day," said Dad. "Let's go back—"

"No!" yelled Stink.

"We can get a cold drink and chill out back at the room until it's time for dinner," said Mum. "And you can look at the shells we found."

"Shells, smells," said Stink. "We can't quit now. Other People are getting close.

Other People are taller than us. And smarter. Other People could win."

"For sure and absolute positive," said Judy.

They went to the antique shop. No hourglass. They checked the library. No hourglass. They went to the museum, where they saw all sorts of shipwreck stuff – but no hourglass.

"What a bust," said Judy.

"At least we got to see real gold," said Stink.

"You mean gold *dust*," said Judy. "C'mon, Stinkerbell. We've been looking for an hourglass for the last *hour*. Even *I* want to go back."

"OK, Poopy Longstocking," said Stink.

⚓ ⚓ ⚓

Back at the inn Stink flopped onto the big bed and stared at the ceiling.

"*Now* who's Poopy Longstocking?" said Judy.

"Yeah, but she had a suitcase full of gold coins," said Stink. "We've got nothing. *Nada.* Zip. Zero."

"Don't give up on the ship now," said Judy. "We only need three more."

"After a rest," said Mum, "how about we get some dinner, then go on the town Ghost Walk? I bought some art supplies in case you want to make rubbings of any of the old gravestones."

Stink sat up. "Will there be dead pirates?"

⚓ ⚓ ⚓

At the first sign of dusk, a group of visitors met in the car park outside the Village Artisan.

"Guess who's following us? I mean, *spying* on us. Tall Boy and Smart Girl! Copycats," Stink hissed.

"Copy kittens," Judy echoed.

A white-haired man with a necktie led the tour. "Almost three hundred years ago, Blackbeard met his death here. They went *chop* – off with his head – then tossed him overboard. Story goes, the headless body swam around the ship seven times before going under." He pointed through the trees to a sandy beach. "Some say if you go out

on Springer's Point at night, you'll see
the ghost of Blackbeard himself, glowing
in the dark, roaming around, looking for
that head."

The small band of people followed
the man up and down Howard Street,
peering over wooden fences into
graveyards, where they were treated
to stories of folks buried on the island:
Old Diver; Edgar the banjo player. They
stopped at three cemeteries sprinkled
with headstones that had ships and

seashells, anchors and arrows, hearts and handshakes.

But not one single hourglass.

At the end of the tour, they came to a small graveyard behind a big white historic house that was now a museum.

Judy was working on a gravestone rubbing of a whale when Stink rushed up to her. "Guess what? I was spying on the You-Know-Whos. I heard Tall Boy say '*X* marks the spot.' Then they both died laughing, like it was a really good joke."

"Weird," said Judy.

"Double weird," Stink agreed. "So I followed them."

"Did you find anything out about an hourglass?" Judy whispered.

"Did I!" Stink pulled out a rolled-up piece of paper from behind his back. When he unrolled it, Judy saw a crayon rubbing of an old pirate grave with an hourglass on it. The hourglass looked like a big *X*.

Here Lies

"*X does* mark the spot," said Judy. "This has to be it, Stink. I feel it in my bones. Let's go and turn it in and get our silver."

Judy and Stink ran around to the front of the house and yanked on the door. It was closed. As in *not open*. As in *locked up tight*.

Stink pressed his nose to the glass, peering in the front window. "We have to break in there or Tall Boy and Smart Girl are going to beat us for sure."

"Stink, it's too late. Nobody's here. We can't just break in—"

"Hey, maybe we could set off the fire alarm!"

"Great idea, Stink – if you want to go to jail."

"Wish I had super-duper, double-quadruple X-ray vision," said Stink. "If there's another clue, I'd see it from here."

"Forget it, Stink. We'll just have to wait till morning."

"Says you," said Stink.

"Says Pirate Rule Number Ten and

a Half: he who breaks into a museum after dark will get locked in the brig, fed to the scurvy rats and end up in Davy Jones's locker. Mad Molly O'Maggot has spoken."

"Drat and bilge bunkle!" said Stink.

As Judy and Stink went back down the steps, a blood-red moon rose in the sky. Twisty branches of the live oaks made spooky shadows across the pavement. An owl hooted. Tree frogs croaked. Judy and Stink nearly jumped out of their skins when they heard a squeaky, creaking sound.

"It's just this rusty old gate, folks," said the tour guide. "Or is it? Folks around these parts have been known

to hear strange sounds: laughs, cries, voices coming from nowhere, flashes of light that can't be explained."

Stink shivered. Judy pulled her arms up into her sweatshirt.

"Let's get out of here," said Stink. "This place gives me the spooks."

"Some pirate," said Judy.

⚓ ⚓ ⚓

When Judy and Stink finally fell asleep that night, visions of hourglasses danced in their heads.

The next morning, they dragged Dad out of bed as soon as they woke up. As he drove them to the old white house, Judy kept an eye out for Tall Boy and Smart Girl.

When they arrived at the house, Stink checked Dad's watch a hundred times. At last, a lady with a red sash and ten hundred keys came to open the door.

"You're up early," she said. "You must be treasure hunters."

"Sure are," said Dad. "Have you had many others?"

"Like maybe possibly a really tall boy?" said Stink. "And a girl who wears glasses and looks super-smart?"

"You're my first customers," said the lady.

Stink unrolled his rubbing of the gravestone with the hourglass and showed it to the lady with the red sash. "Is this it? Did we work it out? Do we get any silver?"

"Yes, yes and yes," said the lady, handing over two silver pieces.

Stink dumped all his coins out on to the counter. "Two, four, six … fifteen! All we need is one more. One!"

"OK, Stink. I can count," said Judy. "But we still have to work out the last and final clue, and it's the hardest. We only have till noon."

"Here you go," said the lady, giving the clue to Judy.

"Let's go back to the inn and get Mum. Then we can all go and eat some breakfast," said Dad.

"I'm not hungry," said Stink. "Read it! Read it!" he cried at Judy.

Judy read the clue:

Clue 5

Sound without ears,
voice without tongue,
rings without fingers,
song without lung.

Hear the sound;
get the lie of the land.
Find the last silver
at the crab's right hand.

"Spitballs and barnacles," said Stink. "It doesn't make any sense. Sound, but no ears? A voice, but no tongue? Not possible."

"Other stuff has a tongue," said Judy. "Like sneakers."

"But sneakers don't have a voice," Stink pointed out.

"Well – bells have rings, but they don't have fingers."

"Great. All we have to do is find a giant talking sneaker bell."

"Or, in your case, a Stinker Bell." Judy cracked herself up.

"What about the crab's right hand?" Stink asked. "It says, 'Find the last silver at the crab's right hand.' Crabs don't even have hands."

"A crab's right hand is a claw, Stink. A crab claw."

"There are millions of crabs on this island, and they all have claws."

"But there's only one place called the Crab's Claw," said Judy, pointing to the map. "It's a restaurant on Ocean View Road."

"Suddenly I'm hungry," said Stink. "Hungry as a shark."

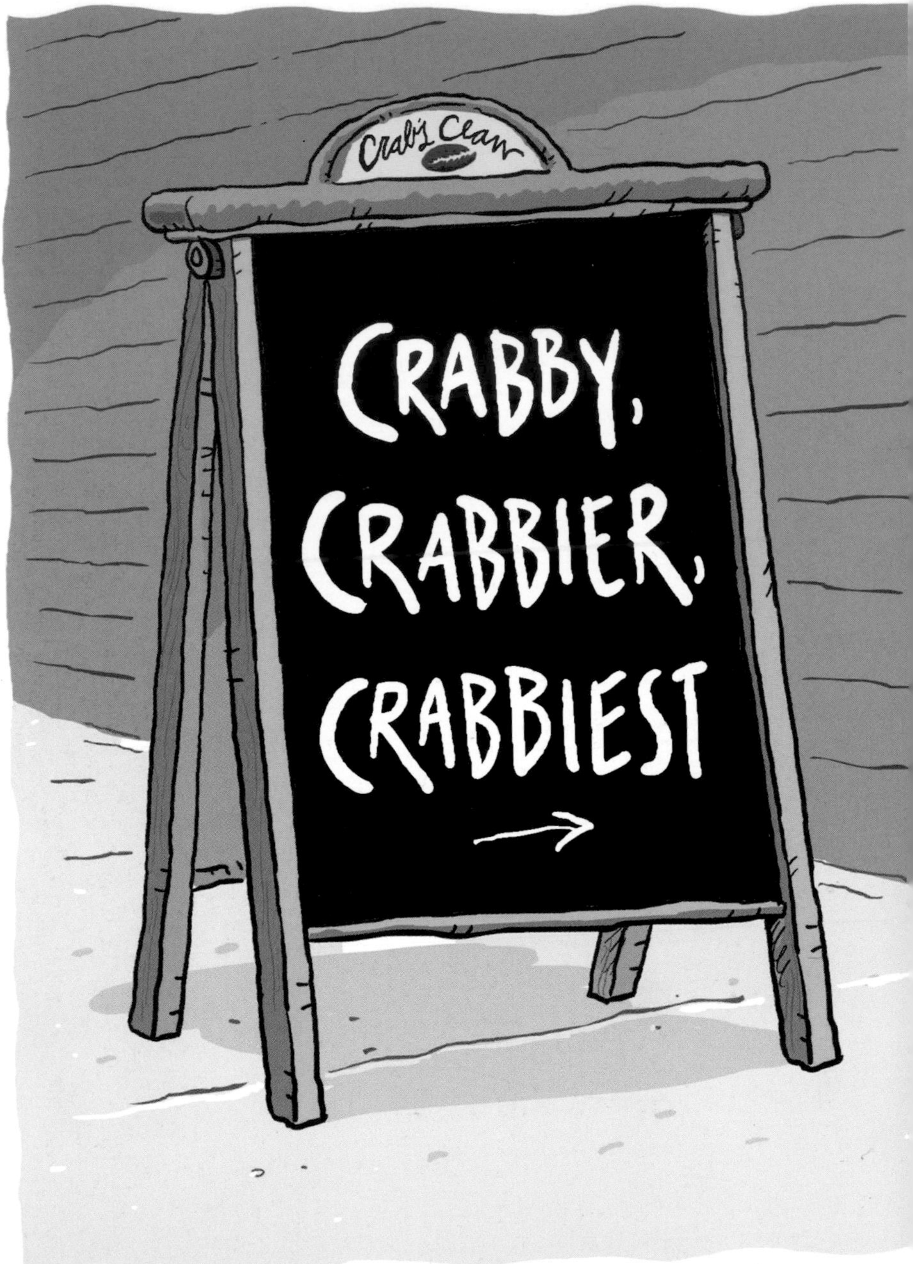
Crab's Claw
CRABBY,
CRABBIER,
CRABBIEST

Before Judy and Stink could step inside the Crab's Claw, out came another family. Tall Boy and Smart Girl! Judy said, "Hi."

"Why did you say hi?" Stink asked when they sat down.

"It just popped out," said Judy.

"Tall Boy and *Crab* Girl are beating our pants off. Did they look like they were just eating breakfast? Or searching for clues? What if they've already found the gold and we're too late?"

"Chill out, Curious George," said Judy. "Believe me, if they'd found it, we'd know." She dug through all the sugar packets at the table and found four with seashells for her collection.

"Let's look for the last piece of eight," Stink urged. "Scurvy Sam said it would be hard. But it has to be here – it just has to."

"Order first," said Mum.

Stink stared at the menu.

Menu

Crab Omelette
Crab Suzette
Crab & Eggs
Benedict
Crab Fritters
Blue Crab Bagel
She-Crab Casserole

"This menu sure is crabby."

"*You* sure are crabby," said Judy.

"You're crabbier," said Stink.

"You're crabbiest," said Judy.

"You're a she-crab," said Stink.

"Well, you're a he-crab," said Judy.

The waiter asked, "What can I get for you folks this morning?"

"A glass of water, please," said Stink.

"Me too," said Judy.

"Kids," said Mum, "you have to eat."

"Order cereal," Judy told Stink. "That's the fastest."

While they waited for their food, Judy and Stink nosed around, searching for the last coin hidden in a crab's claw. There were crabs hanging in nets on the walls.

There were crabby curtains, crab-shaped mirrors, crab door knockers.

"There are ten hundred million crabs in this place," said Judy.

But not one single piece of silver.

"I've got it!" said Stink. "Once I saw this old film called *Mysterious Island,* and these two guys, Ted and Ned or something, walk *right on top* of this evil giant crab under the sand. The crab attacks and grabs Ned—"

"How do you know it was Ned?"

"I'm just saying," said Stink. "Anyway, listen. Ned screams while the other guy ties a rope round one of the giant crab's claws. He flips the crab off a cliff and tosses him into a pool of super-boiling-hot

water. And then they eat him."

"Food's here," Dad called to them.

"So what's your point?" Judy asked.

"My point is that there could be a giant crab hidden under the sand on this island, and in his right claw could be the silver coin. Why didn't I think of it before?"

"Go figure," said Judy.

⚓ ⚓ ⚓

On their way out Stink asked, "Is this the right hand of the crab?"

"No, it's the Crab's Claw," said the lady behind the counter.

"Are you by any chance an Assistant Pirate? Do you have a silver piece of eight hidden somewhere?"

"Not here, I'm afraid," said the lady, shaking her head. "Sorry, kids."

"So what's next?" Dad asked when they got outside.

"Oops, I have to go back," said Judy. "I forgot my sugar packets. And my place mat. I want to save it for my scrapbook."

"Hurry up!" said Stink. "We're almost out of time."

A few minutes later, Judy came rushing out of the restaurant, waving her place mat in the air. "Stink! I think I've found it. Take a look at this." She held out her paper place mat for him to see.

"So? It's a place mat," he said.

"Look at what's *on* the place mat."

Stink looked again. "So? It's a map."

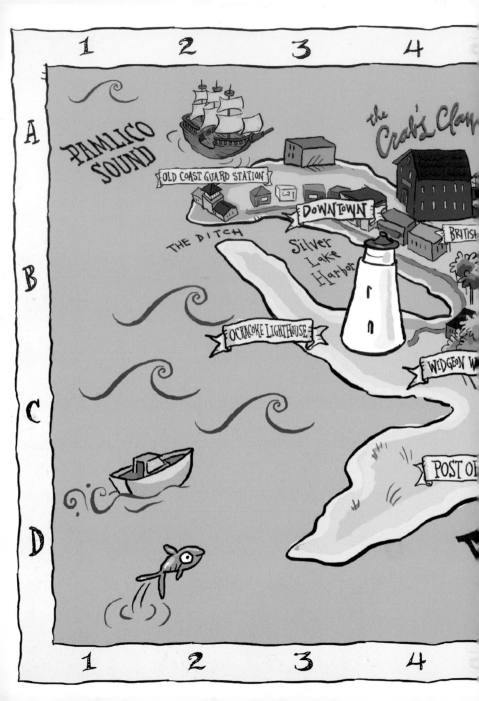

Judy pointed again. "Stop being a Crabby Appleton for one second and look harder."

"So? It's a map of the island."

"It's a map of the island *and* the Atlantic Ocean *and* Pamlico Sound." Judy traced her finger round the tip of land that formed Silver Lake Harbor. "Look at the *shape* of the island."

"So? It looks like—" Finally it hit him. "It looks like a giant crab claw!" Stink shrieked, jumping up and down.

Judy clamped a hand over his mouth. "Tell the whole world, why don't you?"

Dad turned onto Silver Lake Drive, and they followed it round the harbour.

"Take us out as far as you can go, Dad," said Stink.

"Yeah, to the tip of the crab's claw," said Judy.

"We can park at the visitor's centre," Mum suggested.

They got out of the car and looked around. "I see a bunch of kids with maps," Mum said. "They seem to be crossing the boardwalk over to the museum. But the

tip of the island is really the old Coast
Guard Station. It's the one with the bell
outside, down by the water."

"Bell?" said Judy and Stink at the
same time.

"A bell rings," said Stink, "but doesn't
have fingers."

"What do you call that thingy that
hangs inside a bell?"

"A clapper," said Mum.

"Or a tongue," said Dad.

"'Sound without ears,'" said Stink.

"'Voice without tongue,'" said Judy.
"I bet that bell doesn't ring."

"'Cause there's pirate booty in there."
Stink stopped in his tracks. "I think I just
saw Tall Boy and Smart Girl go into the

museum. What if there's another bell in there? The right one?"

But Judy had already taken off.

"Wait for me!" cried Stink.

They stopped in front of a large brass bell. Stink pushed it. "It doesn't ring!"

"But look inside! Look inside!" Judy squealed. Stink stuck his head up inside the bell. "See anything?"

"Dark," said Stink. "Torch!"

Judy dug into Stink's backpack and pulled out the torch. She stuck her head inside the bell and shone the torch all around.

Suddenly the beam of light hit something shiny. A shimmer. A sparkle. Silver! A shiny silver coin was duct-taped to the inside of the bell.

"Eureka!" said Judy.

"Mum! Dad!" yelled Stink. "We've struck gold!"

"Well, really we've struck silver," said Judy. "But that means we win, win, win!"

Judy and Stink screamed and hugged each other. People near by stared, squirrels skittered and seagulls took flight.

Judy and Stink jumped around and shouted until they were all out of breath, and collapsed in a fit of giggles. Stink got the hiccups because he was laughing so hard. "I feel – *hic* – like I've won – *hic* – the Olympics!" he said. *"HIC!"*

"The Hiccup Olympics," said Judy.

A guy from the Coast Guard Station came up and shook hands with them. "Base to Scurvy Sam," he said into a walkie-talkie. "Come in, Scurvy Sam. We have a couple of winners."

Mum and Dad caught up and peered at the silver coin.

"I can't believe we beat Tall Boy and Smart Girl," said Stink. "Just in time too."

"It's great that you kids stuck it out and didn't give up," said Dad.

"See what can happen when you two work together?" said Mum.

"Two brains are better than one," said Judy.

"Especially when it's Scurvy-Stink-and-Mad-Molly-O'Maggot brains," Stink said, tapping his head.

⚓ ⚓ ⚓

Scurvy Stink and Mad Molly reported to Pirate Headquarters just before noon. A small crowd of people had gathered, waiting.

Stink and Judy ran up to Scurvy Sam. Stink opened his pouch and counted out all sixteen pieces of eight. Scurvy Sam's eyes lit up brighter than the firecrackers that Blackbeard was famous for having in his beard. "Well, blow me down. If it ain't Mad Molly and Scurvy Stink. Ain't you two o' the smartest urchins on the Outer Banks!"

Scurvy Sam climbed aboard his ship and clanged the bell twelve times. "Avast, me hearties! We have us two winners!"

After a big speech, Scurvy Sam climbed down and went up to Judy and Stink. He raised their hands in the air, then danced a funny hornpipe. The crowd clapped and hooted.

"Now tell us, fer all to hear," he said. "How'd ye do it, me mateys? What's yer secret? *Arrr.*"

"Just super-duper brain power," said Stink, tapping his head. "And a trusty-dusty survival kit."

"And a little luck," Judy said. "Even though Stink almost got us thrown in jail."

The crowd broke into laughter.

Scurvy Sam presented Judy and Stink each with a shiny gold doubloon. Stink's had a skull and crossbones and said *1587* on the back.

"Rare," said Judy. "Mine has pictures of Blackbeard *and* Anne Bonny!"

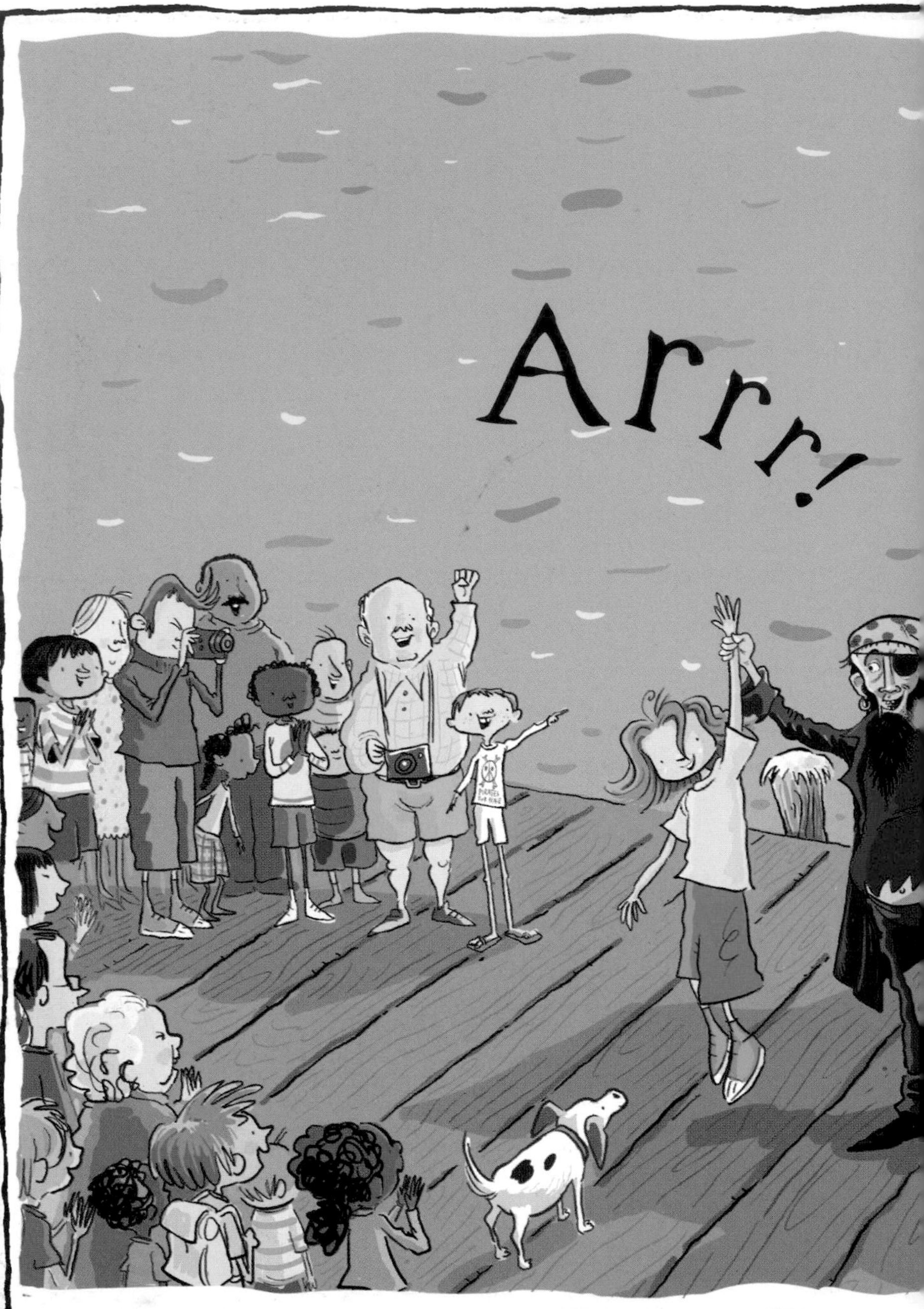
Arrr!

"Whoa, it's like a *gold* silver dollar," said Stink. "Is it real?"

"It'll break yer teeth if ye bite it."

"It's not cursed, is it?" Stink asked.

Scurvy Sam winked. "Would an old sea dog like me curse a fellow pirate?" He turned back to the crowd.

"That be it, mateys. Thanks be to ye one and all for makin' the Third Annual Pirate Island Treasure Hunt such a dandy hoot and a holler. Now, mind ye, don't be leavin' without yer pirate booty! Treasure for all!"

The Assistant Pirates passed out goody bags while Scurvy Sam shook hands and waved goodbye to all the treasure hunters.

"I told you it was the bell," said a Girl voice.

"I know you did, but you never said which bell, and there was one inside the museum!" said a Boy voice.

Judy's eyes grew wide. Stink hiccuped. Tall Boy and Smart Girl!

"You're so lucky," Smart Girl said to Judy and Stink. "We came all the way from Maine, and we really wanted to win."

"We tried really hard. We were sure we had it," said Tall Boy.

"Wow!" said Smart Girl, eyeing Stink's doubloon. "Sure is shiny."

"Yeah," said Stink. "There's only one thing better than gold."

"What could be better than gold?" Judy asked.

"A ride on a for-real pirate ship!" said Stink.

"I'd give anything to ride on a pirate ship," said Tall Boy.

Judy looked at Stink. Stink looked at Judy. She couldn't help feeling funny about beating them. She could tell Stink felt bad too.

"Actually, we can't go for a ride on the pirate ship after all," Judy said.

"What?!" said Smart Girl and Tall Boy at the same time.

"Have ye lost yer senses?" said Scurvy Sam, overhearing them.

"Not alone, anyway. We'd be breaking Pirate Rule Number Two," said Judy.

"That's right!" Stink piped up. "Pirate Rule Two says that if you find treasure, you have to share it – even-steven."

"By jiggers, they be right!" said Scurvy Sam. "And the punishment for breakin' Pirate Rule Number Two be marooning ye on a desert island with nothin' but bugs for grub."

"You've got to come with us," Stink told Tall Boy and Smart Girl.

"Save us from eating bugs," said Judy.

"Besides," said Stink, "you guys kind of helped us win."

"We did?" asked Smart Girl, crinkling her nose.

"We saw you guys looking through your binoculars, so we looked too. That's how we found the sign of the pirate."

"But we found it 'cause of *you*," said Tall Boy. "We saw you pointing up at the sign in front of the art shop, and that made us look."

"But Stink heard *you* saying '*X* marks the spot' at the graveyard, so he followed you," Judy said. "That's how we found the hourglass."

Smart Girl looked at Scurvy Sam. "Can we?"

"I'd be mighty honoured to have two more pirates aboard, me beauty."

"You mean it?" asked Smart Girl.

"I swear it, in the name of Davy Jones."

"OK, you can come," said Stink. "But only on one condition."

"What's that?" asked Tall Boy.

"You have to clean the poop deck!" said Stink.

"*Arrgh!*" moaned Tall Boy and Smart Girl.

"Kidding!" Stink said, and everybody cracked up. Stink laughed the loudest – a laugh that could be heard on the wind, across the seven seas and back again ... a laugh that was sure to haunt Pirate Island for years to come.

PIRATE RULES

1. Every crew member has an equal vote and an equal share of food and drink on the ship.

2. All crew members have an equal share in treasure.

3. There is to be no playing cards or rolling dice for money.

4. Lights and candles shall be out by eight o'clock each night, or else!

5. Every crew member must have a pistol and a cutlass ready for use at all times.

6. No girl or woman shall be allowed on board ship. Break this rule and die!

7. Deserting ship in battle shall result in death or marooning.

8. No fighting is allowed on board ship. All quarrels must be settled on shore.

9. There is to be no talk of jumping ship until everyone has shared at least one thousand pounds.

10. The ship's musician shall rest on Sundays.